MW01016313

Room for Rabbit

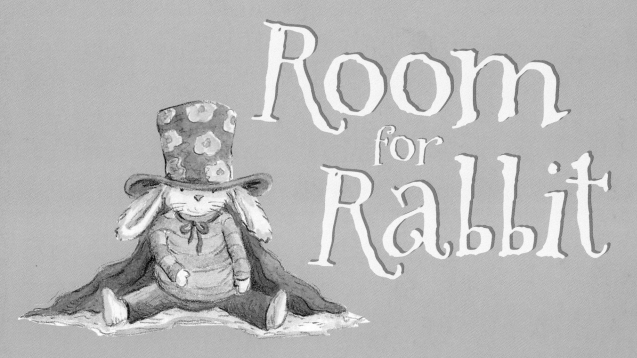

by Roni Schotter

illustrated by Cyd Moore

Clarion Books ❦ New York

Clarion Books
a Houghton Mifflin Company imprint
215 Park Avenue South, New York, NY 10003

The illustrations were rendered in watercolor.
The text was set in 16-point Berling Roman.

www.houghtonmifflinbooks.com

Printed in Singapore.

Library of Congress Cataloging-in-Publication Data
Schotter, Roni.
Room for Rabbit / by Roni Schotter ; illustrated by Cyd Moore.
p.   cm.
Summary: Now that Papa is remarried, his house seems very crowded, and Kara
wonders if there is still enough room there for her and her toy Rabbit.
ISBN 0-618-18183-0 (alk. paper)
[1. Remarriage—Fiction. 2. Toys—Fiction.]
I. Moore, Cyd, ill. II. Title.
PZ7.S3765 Ro 2003   [E]—dc21   2002009036

TWP   10 9 8 7 6 5 4 3 2 1

Papa is coming to pick up Kara and take her to his house, so Mama and Kara pack up her knapsack. Mama packs a special love bug she has cut out of paper for Kara, covered with kisses. Kara packs her favorite books. Most important of all, Kara packs Rabbit, who rides on top. "You stay with me and go wherever I go," Kara reminds him. "Otherwise, there is too much missing!"

Knock, knock. It's Papa with his Peggy. Papa used to be married to Mama, but now he is married to Peggy. At Papa and Peggy's wedding, Kara wore a long dress and carried a basket of flowers. A basket of flowers and Rabbit, of course.

Papa lifts Kara high into the air. He's wearing the warm, woolly sweater Kara loves so much. "How's my flying flower girl? Ready to go, Sweet Piccolo?" he asks.

"Ready." Kara giggles, but first she hugs Mama and covers her with goodbye kisses.

Mama whispers a secret message in Kara's ear. "Take good care of Rabbit and my love bug," she tells her, "and don't forget to have fun with Papa and Peggy."

"Of course I won't forget," Kara promises. "Silly Mama!"

At Papa's house, Kara and Rabbit stick close together. Papa's house feels different now that Peggy lives there. Kara keeps Mama's love bug right next to her. Before, there was Papa's dog, Popcorn. Now there is also Peggy's dog, Carrots. Before, there were Papa's things and Kara's things. Now there are also Peggy's things. *Lots* of Peggy's things!

Peggy makes clothing for people who act in plays. Now ties—wide and mini, long and skinny—hang like noodles from the cabinet where Papa and Kara keep their favorite treats. Now hats—flowered and floppy, silly and sloppy—tumble from the chest where Kara keeps her toys.

When Kara and Rabbit try to lie on the couch where she and Papa snuggle to tell each other stories, they can't—because it's hidden under mountains of gloves and hills of scarves. When they try to sit in the special chair Papa made for them, they find it's covered with Peggy's capes. Rabbit leans up against Kara's ear and whispers a question only Kara can hear, "Is there room for me?" Kara isn't sure.

When no one's looking, Kara shoves Peggy's capes aside and they fall to the ground in a big puddle. Peggy picks up the capes and hangs them over a lamp. "Here's something special I made for Rabbit," she says. It's a cape—a silky, shiny one with Rabbit's name sewn on it. But when Peggy gives it to Kara, Rabbit whispers once more in Kara's ear.

"Rabbit says thank you," Kara tells Peggy, "but he'd rather not wear it."

Suddenly, everything is still in Papa's house. No one moves. Popcorn stays in one corner and Carrots in another.

Finally, Papa speaks. "How about a game of hide-and-seek?"
He pulls one of Peggy's scarves from the couch and ties it
over his eyes. "On the count of ten—ready or not, here I
come!" he shouts. "Ten . . . nine . . ."

Peggy doesn't know the best hiding places in Papa's
house, so she just kneels behind the couch. So easy to see!

Where should Kara and Rabbit hide? Under the bed?
Behind the curtains? In the broom closet! Kara opens
the door and is showered with shoes. Shoes with straps.
Shoes with bows. Flat shoes. Fat shoes. Shoes that look
like cat shoes! Peggy's shoes are everywhere.

"Not enough room," Rabbit says.

"Five . . . four . . . three . . ." Papa calls out.

Kara puts Rabbit down and pushes the shoes aside to make a space. "Ready or not!" Papa yells, so Kara hurries to squeeze in, then shuts the door.

Inside the closet, Kara listens as Papa goes hunting. He finds Peggy first, of course. Kara hears Peggy and Papa. They laugh and laugh together. Kara feels lonely in the closet. Has Papa forgotten her? She rubs Mama's love bug and reaches down to hug Rabbit, but when she does . . . Rabbit isn't there!

Where's Rabbit?

Kara throws open the door and tumbles out of the
crowded closet. She looks for Rabbit. Where *is* he? *There*
he is, on the floor, looking sad and forgotten among Peggy's
shoes. "Not enough room," Kara hears him mumble.

"Me-oh-my," Papa calls out, seeing Kara. "Who's that I spy?"

"We're *not playing!*" Kara shouts.

"Why not?" Papa asks.

Rabbit whispers in Kara's ear. "Rabbit says it's *too crowded* here!" Kara tells Papa. "There isn't enough room for him now that you and Peggy are married."

"What else does Rabbit say?" Papa asks quietly.

"He says no one cares about him anymore," Kara answers.

Papa carries Rabbit and Kara over to the couch. He takes them into his big, soft lap, puts his thick, woolly arms around them, and hugs them oh-so-tight. Kara closes her eyes. She feels like a tiny bird in Papa's lap nest. For a long time Papa doesn't say anything. Then Kara feels more arms around her. They are long and strong and Kara knows they belong to Peggy. "There will *always* be room for you and Rabbit," Papa says, "and now that Peggy is here, there will be more laps to sit in . . ."

". . . and more arms to hug with," Peggy whispers. Her arms feel like extra tree branches wrapped around Kara and Rabbit, holding them tight in Papa's lap nest. "But Rabbit is right. There *isn't* enough room! I have too many things. What shall we do?" Now Peggy looks sad.

For a while, no one speaks, not even Rabbit. Then Papa says, "I know!" He jumps up, takes an old screen from behind the couch, and starts to pile Peggy's shoes behind it.

Then Kara says, "I know!" She jumps up, removes her coat from the coat tree, and hangs Peggy's scarves from its posts.

Then she and Papa and Peggy and Rabbit get to work. . . . Even Popcorn and Carrots help. . . . They throw Peggy's costumes. They stow Peggy's costumes. They fold and furl and twirl Peggy's costumes. Last of all, Papa lifts Kara up so she can put a stack of Peggy's hats on the tippy-top of the coat tree. Kara laughs. The coat tree looks like a giant wearing many hats!

But Peggy still has one pile of clothing left. From it, she pulls a scarf that sparkles with beads as bright as winking stars, and a hat with a velvet ribbon and a long, curling feather. "These are for you, Kara," Peggy says. "From me."

Kara *wants* to put them on, but she isn't sure that she should. What will Rabbit say? Rabbit whispers his answer in Kara's ear. It's OK, he tells her. Then he whispers one thing more.

"What is he saying?" Peggy and Papa ask.

"He says he'd like to wear his cape now and one of Peggy's hats . . . if that's OK."

"Of course it's OK!" Peggy says, handing Kara Rabbit's clothes. She pulls one of her floppy hats from the pile, and puts it on Papa. He looks like a clown! She yanks a green scarf made of feathers and a big brown hat from the pile, and puts them on. She looks like a sea captain! Peggy even has hats for Popcorn and Carrots.

Papa smiles. Peggy smiles. Kara smiles. From under Peggy's hat, it looks as if Rabbit is smiling. Kara thinks about her promise to Mama. She has kept it. She imagines that Mama is smiling, too.

Soon it will be time for Kara to pack up and go back
to Mama's house, but first, under the light of the lamp,
she and Rabbit and Papa and Peggy—even Popcorn and
Carrots—crowd cozy on the couch to tell each other
stories. "Does everyone have enough room?" Papa asks.

Kara looks down at Rabbit in her lap. Popcorn's head
rests on his back. Peggy's hand wraps round his feet and
somewhere, squashed beneath, lies one of Papa's woolly
arms. Rabbit whispers an answer in Kara's ear. "Plenty of
room," he says.

When she is back at Mama's, Kara gives Mama her gift—some pretend eyelashes from Papa and Peggy's house. Then she and Mama and Rabbit pile pillows on the floor and play their favorite love game—Nestle-and-Nuzzle.

Mama's house doesn't feel as full as Papa and Peggy's does. "Papa has Peggy," Kara says, nestling her nose in Mama's soft neck. "Who do you have?"

"I have you and Rabbit and *so much* love that it fills every corner of this house," Mama answers, nuzzling her nose in Kara's curly hair. Mama's long eyelashes feel like tiny butterflies. They tickle Kara and make her smile.

Rabbit whispers a question. "Rabbit wants to know, what if *you* got married one day, like Papa? Would there be enough room?"

"Silly Rabbit!" Mama says to Kara, "what shall we tell him?"

"That there will *always* be room," Kara says, and she nestles even closer to Mama and hugs Rabbit tight between them.

"What a smart Rabbit!" Mama says, and covers Kara with kisses.